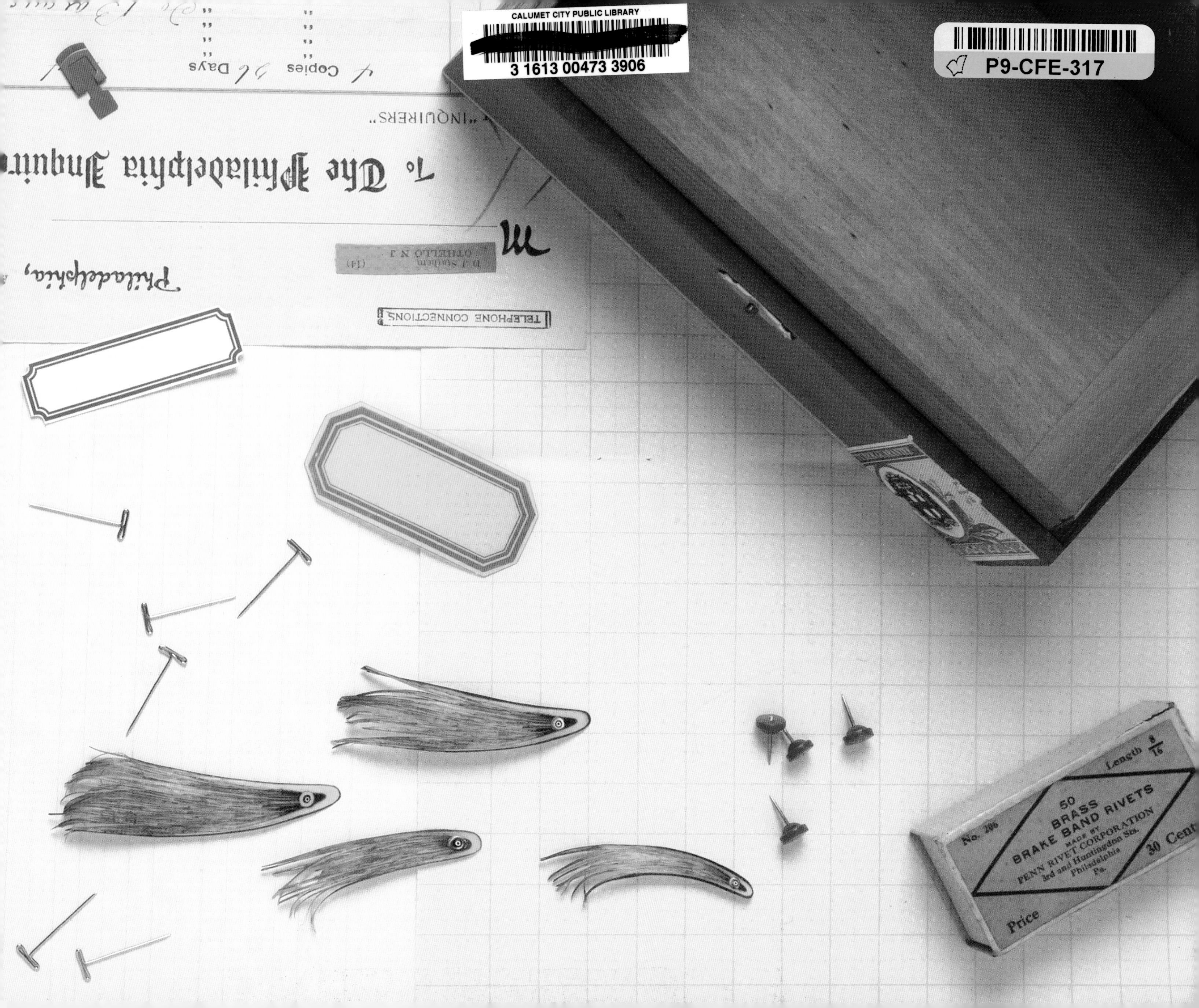

CALUMET CITY PUBLIC LIBRARY
3 1613 00473 3906
P9-CFE-317

J
811
PRE

S·T·A·R·D·I·N·E·S

SWIM HIGH ACROSS THE SKY

and other poems

* * * * *

by **JACK PRELUTSKY**

illustrated by **CARIN BERGER**

GREENWILLOW BOOKS
An Imprint of HarperCollins*Publishers*

CALUMET CITY PUBLIC LIBRARY

To VAD for your leap of faith, to BB for every little thing,
to Joseph Cornell (of course!), and, as always, to Thea
—C. B.

Stardines Swim High Across the Sky and Other Poems
Text copyright © 2012 by Jack Prelutsky
Illustrations copyright © 2012 by Carin Berger

All rights reserved. Manufactured in China. For information address HarperCollins Children's Books, a division of HarperCollins Publishers, 10 East 53rd Street, New York, NY 10022.
www.harpercollinschildrens.com

The miniature dioramas in this book are assemblages created using a combination of cut paper, found ephemera, vintage engravings (which were scanned, manipulated in Photoshop, and then printed out), beeswax, wire, thread, and wood. Once each piece was made, it was then photographed digitally to prepare the full-color art.

The text type is Courier.
Photography by Porter Gillespie

Library of Congress Cataloging-in-Publication Data

Prelutsky, Jack.
Stardines swim high across the sky and other poems
by Jack Prelutsky ; illustrations by Carin Berger.
p. cm.
"Greenwillow Books."
ISBN 978-0-06-201464-1 (trade bdg.)—ISBN 978-0-06-201465-8 (lib. bdg.)
[1. Imaginary creatures—Juvenile poetry. 2. Children's poetry, American.]
I. Berger, Carin, ill. II. Title.
PS3566.R36S73 2012 811'.54—dc23 2011025993
First Edition

Greenwillow Books

For Madelyn and Thomas
—J. P.

With great gratitude
to Porter
—C. B.

CONTENTS

S t A R D i N E s

S T A R D I N E S swim high across the sky,
And brightly shine as they glide by.
In giant schools, their brilliant lights
Illuminate the darkest nights.

/////

When other creatures are in bed,
S T A R D I N E S still twinkle overhead.
In silence, these nocturnal fish
Are set to grant the slightest wish.

STARDINES
FIG. 44
FIG 292.
FIG. 245
FIG. 260
FIG 17
FIG. 147
FIG. 22
FIG. 321
FIG. 36

STAR-deens

10
Bluffaloes
382
B

BluFFaLoEs

B L U F F A L O E S are bulky beasts,
Preposterously large.
Their demeanor is imposing,
They appear to be in charge.

* * *

Despite their size and attitude,
They're neither fierce nor tough,
And B L U F F A L O E S just run away
If you should call their bluff.

/////

BLUFF-a-lows

SWAP-uh-teez

SwAPitIs

SWAPITIS meet every day
To put their goods out on display.
No sooner have they set up shop,
Than SWAPITIS begin to swap.
They've all amassed assorted things,
Like tennis racquets with no strings,
Like busted bikes, old moldy boots,
And out-of-fashion three-piece suits.

SWAPITIS have endless stocks
Of worn-out socks and broken clocks,
Of warped guitars, chipped bongo drums,
And slightly cracked aquariums.
Back and forth within the woods
They trade for one another's goods,
Exchanging wingless model planes
For misassembled plastic trains.

They barter dented baseball bats
For oddly decorated hats,
For unattractive broken beads,
Or rusty tools that no one needs.
At dusk, when it's too dark to see,
They pack their wares reluctantly
And wish they didn't have to stop,
For SWAPITIS just love to swap.

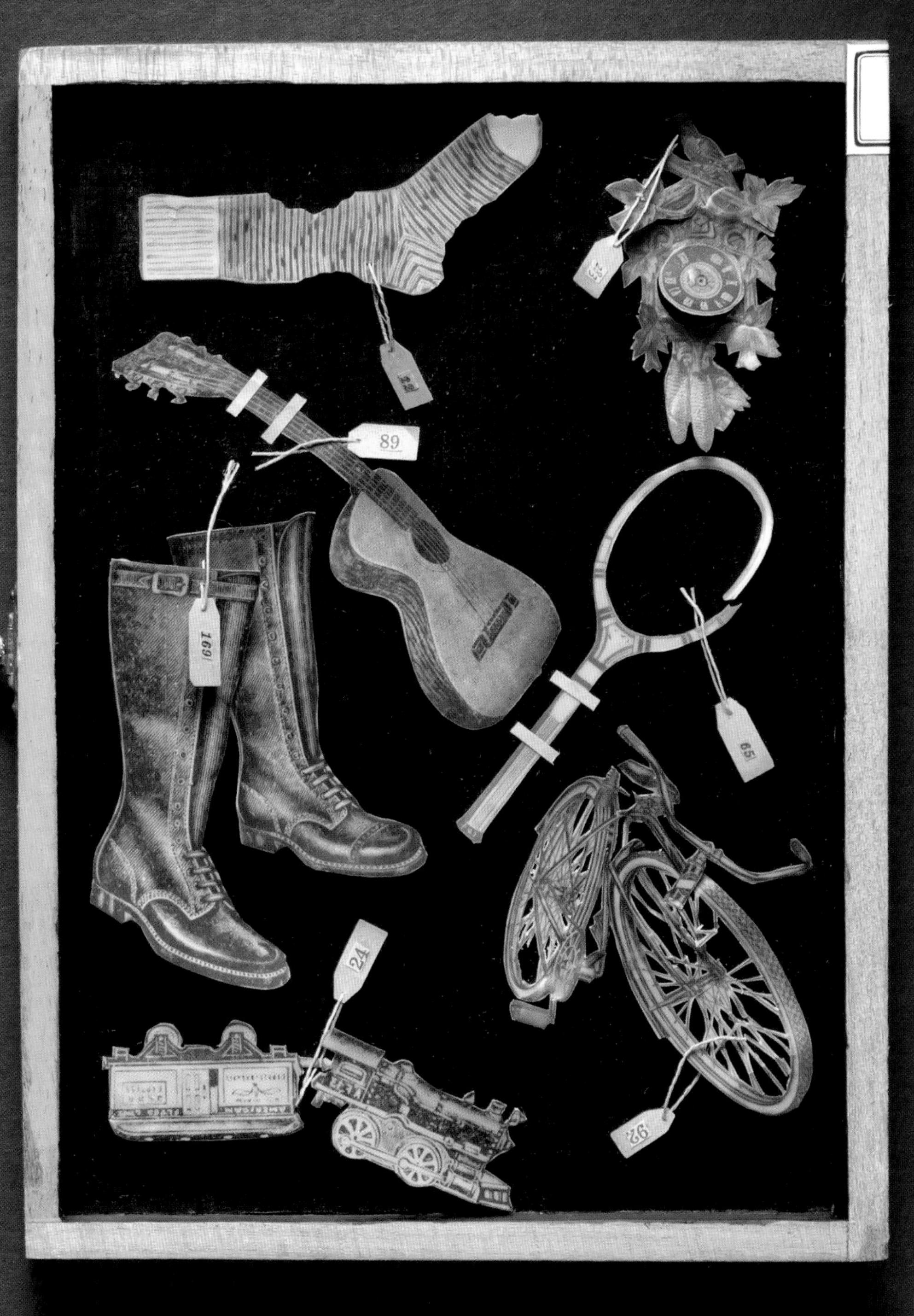

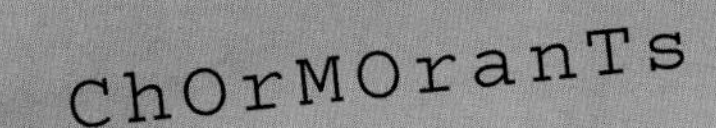

C H O R M O R A N T S are busy birds
That toil from sun to sun.
They labor over senseless chores
They're certain must be done.
They work at this, they work at that,
And never think to ask
If they accomplish anything
With any pointless task.

C H O R M O R A N T S are serious
And have no use for jest.
They feel it is their destiny
To rarely ever rest.
They're strangers to frivolity
And neither sing nor dance.
Their days are endless drudgery—
Poor boring C H O R M O R A N T S.

* * *

CHORE-mor-ants

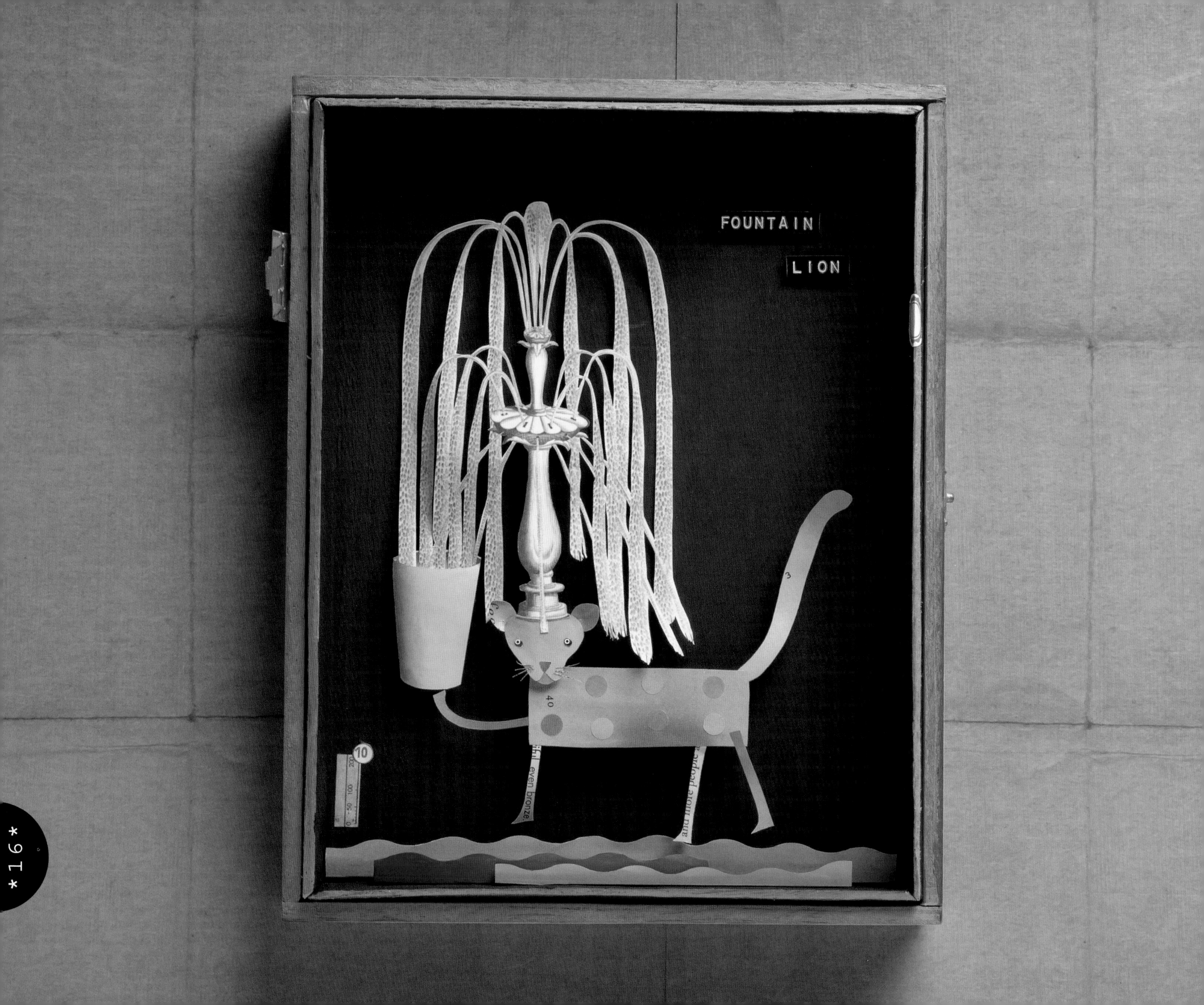
FOUNTAIN
LION
10
even bronze

FOuNtaIN
LiONs

FOUNTAIN LIONS, lithe and lean,
Add gaiety to any scene.
The only lions no one dreads,
They all have fountains on their heads.
They are not predatory beasts
Upon the prowl for easy feasts.
Instead, with evident delight,
They run their fountains day and night.

Of course, they have to drink and drink
To keep those fountains in the pink.
When water is in short supply,
Those FOUNTAIN LIONS soon run dry.
But, as a rule, they drink their fill,
Then spout with artistry and skill.
At sending up an aqueous stream,
FOUNTAIN LIONS reign supreme.

* * *

FOUN-tin lions

S L O B S T E R S are slovenly,
S L O B S T E R S are crude.
S L O B S T E R S love mashing
And smushing their food.
Their sense of decorum
Is woefully small.
S L O B S T E R S don't have
Many manners at all.

* * *

S L O B S T E R S don't seem
To be happy unless
They're dropping their supper
And making a mess.
They're simply so sloppy
We have to conclude
That S L O B S T E R S are slovenly,
S L O B S T E R S are crude.

/////

SLOB-stirs

PLAN-duz

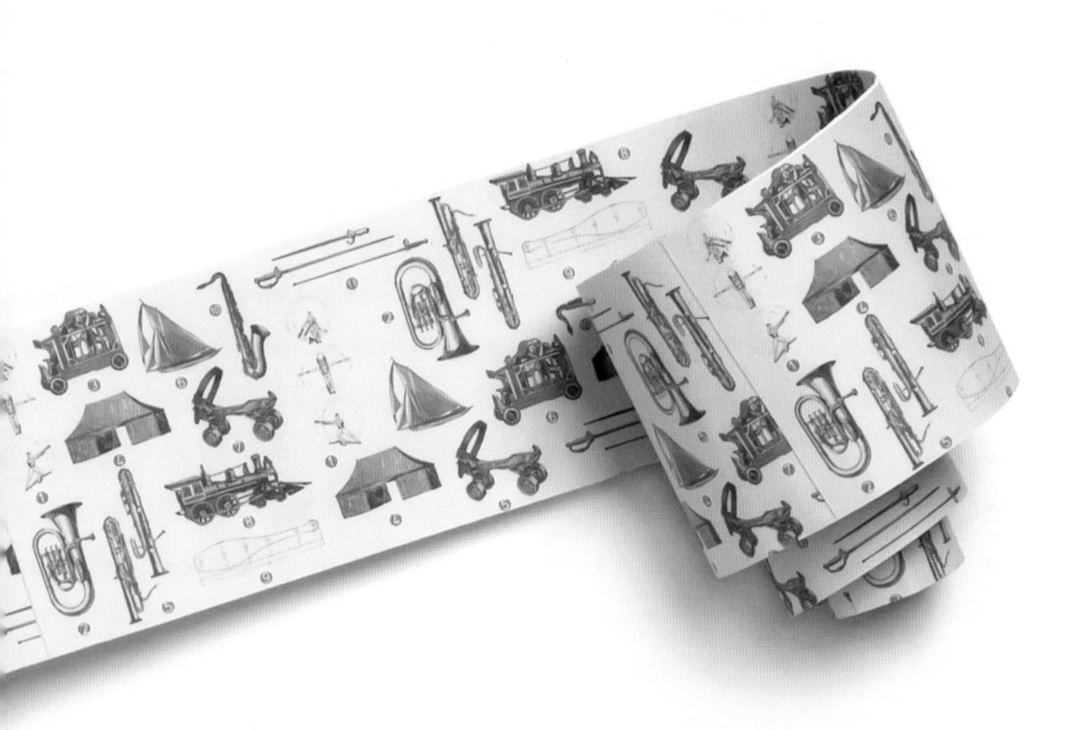

P L a N d a S

P L A N D A S sit around all day,
Planning what to do.
Their plans amount to nothing,
For they never see them through.
They plan to run a marathon
Or take a railroad trip.
They plan to cross the ocean
On a wooden sailing ship.

They plan to learn to roller-skate,
To juggle, and to fence.
They plan to go to clown school
And cavort in circus tents.
They plan to play the saxophone
And form their own brass bands. . . .
But P L A N D A S never do these things—
They just keep making plans.

3 1613 00473 3906

CALUMET CITY PUBLIC LIBRARY

JOLLYFISH are radiant,
Ebullient blobs of mirth,
With merry dispositions
From the moment of their birth.
Though they know their every motion
Is dependent on the tides,
They laugh with such abandon
That they almost split their sides.

* * *

Their humor is infectious,
And as aimlessly they drift,
Their buoyant effervescence
Gives the neighborhood a lift.
JOLLYFISH possess the gift
Of fundamental glee—
There's no creature half as happy
At the bottom of the sea.

JOH-lee-fish

The SobCat

The SOBCAT is sad
As a feline can be
And spends its time crying
Continuously.
It has no real reason
To be so morose.
It's simply its nature
To act lachrymose.

That miserable SOBCAT's
Been moaning for years,
Sitting alone,
Weeping copious tears.
Because it delights
In its own misery,
The SOBCAT is sad
As a feline can be.

SOB-cat

MaGPiPEs

M A G P I P E S sound unpleasant—
They've a tendency to drone.
Their voices are a nasal,
Cacophonic monotone.
They self-inflate their feathered chests
Until they're filled with air,
Then on and on those noisy birds
Monotonously blare.

/////

Nothing but a M A G P I P E
Likes the sounds a MAGPIPE makes.
At best you can describe them
As unmusical mistakes.
Don't listen to a M A G P I P E
If you have another choice.
Consider yourself lucky
If you never hear its voice.

* * *

MAG-pipe

TATTLESNAKE
TATTLE TATTLE TATTLE TATTLE TATTLE TATTLE TATTLE TATTLE

TAT-ul-snake

TATTLESNAKE,
TATTLESNAKE,
Overly keen
To tattle repeatedly—
Truly you're mean.
You're nosy, annoying,
You're venomous, vile.
You don't mind your business,
We don't like your style.

TATTLESNAKE,
TATTLESNAKE,
Making us moan,
Tattling all day,
Leaving no one alone.
Why must you tattle,
And what makes you feel
That anyone cares
About things you reveal?

TATTLESNAKE,
TATTLESNAKE,
Acting so wrong,
Sticking your snout
Where it doesn't belong.
We think your comeuppance
Is long overdue
And hope someday soon
Someone tattles on you.

* * *

CIRCLES
CURVES
A = AREA
d = DIAMETER
r = RADIUS
FORMULAS
triangles

BRaInDeeR

B R A I N D E E R are very clever,
B R A I N D E E R are very wise.
Their brains are very wrinkled
And of a massive size.
Their minds are overflowing
With extreme intelligence.
B R A I N D E E R have lots of knowledge,
B R A I N D E E R have lots of sense.

* * *

With endless perseverance
They serenely mill about,
Reflecting on the universe
And figuring it out.
But, sadly, they cannot convey
A solitary thought,
For B R A I N D E E R cannot speak nor write—
Their thinking is for naught.

/////

BRAIN-deer

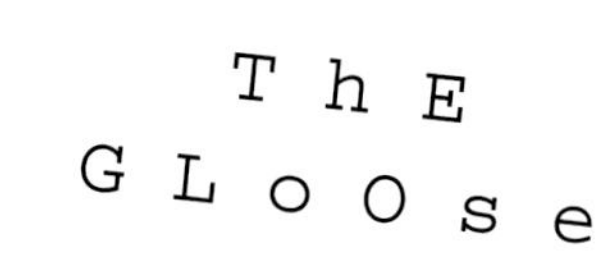

The GLOOSE may be the weirdest bird
That ever took to wing.
It has an odd propensity
To stick to anything.
It often backs into a tree
And instantly adheres,
So then it honks and honks and honks
Till help at last appears.

The GLOOSE is so adhesive
That to free it from its plight
Requires a lot of people
Pulling with a lot of might.
Sometimes it takes a football team
To pry the creature loose.
The conclusion's inescapable—
It's hard to be the GLOOSE.

ROGERS
FAMOUS
LIQUID
GLUE
EVERY DROP
STE-FIX
THE GLUE THAT GRIPS
A Pure Vegetable Glue
DOUBLE STRENGTH
14
98
GLOOSE

GLOOSE

PANTEATERS eat pants
Anytime, anywhere.
The cloth doesn't matter—
PANTEATERS don't care.
On trousers of cotton,
Silk, linen, or wool,
PANTEATERS keep chewing
Until they are full.

They eat polyester
And nylon with zest.
There's no single fabric
PANTEATERS like best.
They gnaw every pocket
And belt loop and cuff.
It often takes hours
Till they've had enough.

Their diet's unchanging,
Except for dessert,
For then they may tackle
A sweater or shirt.
But most of the time,
If they have half a chance,
PANTEATERS eat nothing
But mountains of pants.

PANT-ee-ters

WeDGeHogs

W E D G E H O G S are triangular.
W E D G E H O G S are benign.
W E D G E H O G S are considerate.
W E D G E H O G S wait in line.

W E D G E H O G S, when they wander,
Never wander very far.
W E D G E H O G S always feel at home
Exactly where they are.

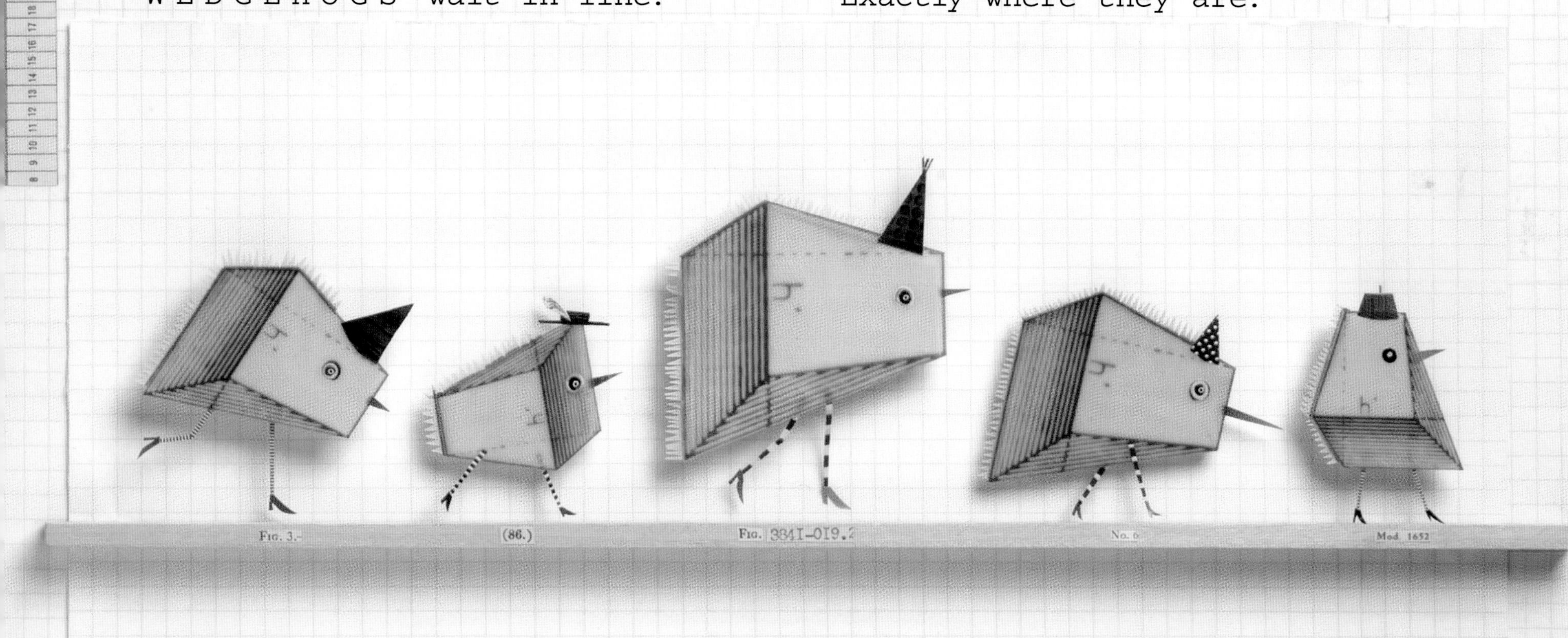

WEDGE-hogs

NO. 2249

B
BarD
BLACK INK
BARDVARKS
17
658.5
No. 95046

BaRDvaRkS

BARDVARKS think they're poets
And persist in writing rhyme.
Their words are uninspired
And a total waste of time.
But BARDVARKS do not know this,
So not only do they write
With unbearable pretension—
They incessantly recite.

BARDVARKS have no talent
For composing simple verse.
They don't improve with practice
And in fact are getting worse.
Undeterred, they keep on writing
And reciting every day.
That's why BARDVARKS are a problem—
You can't make them go away.

BARD-varx

Dennisons
No. 205